To Toby

Library and Archives Canada Cataloguing in Publication

Beck, Andrea, 1956-
Pierre Le Poof! / Andrea Beck.
ISBN 978-1-55469-028-2

I. Title.
PS8553.E2948P44 2009   jC813'.54   C2009-901663-X

Summary: Pierre, a pampered poodle, is torn between his love for his
doting owner and his dream of running wild in the park.

First published in the United States, 2009
Library of Congress Control Number: 2009924733

Orca Book Publishers gratefully acknowledges the support for
its publishing programs provided by the following agencies:
the Government of Canada through the Book Publishing Industry
Development Program and the Canada Council for the Arts,
and the Province of British Columbia through the BC Arts
Council and the Book Publishing Tax Credit.

Cover and interior artwork by Andrea Beck
Design by Teresa Bubela

ORCA BOOK PUBLISHERS   ORCA BOOK PUBLISHERS
PO Box 5626, Stn. B   PO Box 468
Victoria, BC Canada   Custer, WA USA
V8R 6S4   98240-0468

www.orcabook.com
Printed and bound in Canada.

12 11 10 09   •   4 3 2 1

Pierre Le Poof!

written and illustrated by ANDREA BECK

ORCA BOOK PUBLISHERS

Pierre Le Poof was a pedigreed pooch, and every morning he sat nicely while Miss Murphy puffed his pom-poms.

"One day you'll win the championship," she would coo.

Pierre loved Miss Murphy, but he didn't care about championships. He liked to jump up to his seat in the big bay window and watch the dogs in the park.

He wanted to be like them!

The dogs in the park didn't have silly haircuts, and they didn't wear clothes or diamond-studded collars.

Pierre tried all kinds of ways to flatten his pom-poms, but they always sprang up again. And when he hid his coat, hat and boots, Miss Murphy would find them in time for his walks.

Pierre was in training for the poodle championship.
Every day after breakfast he ran on the treadmill.
On Tuesdays he went to the School for Show Pups,
and on Thursdays he went to Poochelli's Pet Parlor
for a shampoo.

While he was being puffed and fluffed, Pierre imagined
running with the wind in his long tangled fur. He chased
squirrels, dug holes and rolled in any stinky thing he pleased.

At home, Pierre kept one eye on the front door and the other on the fire-escape window. He figured if he timed it right, he could slip out to the park for an hour or two while Miss Murphy watched her afternoon TV show.

But in the evenings, Pierre hopped into Miss Murphy's lap, and they curled up in their favorite armchair. Pierre forgot all about sneaking out, because Pierre loved Miss Murphy more than any park on earth.

One nippy fall day, Miss Murphy puffed Pierre to perfection. She put on her hat and pink pom-pomed scarf. Then she and Pierre took a cab to a big stone building on the other side of town.

All the dogs from his Tuesday class were inside.

"We're practicing for tomorrow's dog show, Pierre," said Miss Murphy. "It's the championship!"

Pierre loved to see Miss Murphy smile. So he walked perfectly, he stood perfectly and he held his head just the right way.

When he finished his routine, everyone clapped, Miss Murphy beamed and Pierre wagged his tail. But while Miss Murphy was chatting, Pierre noticed a door to the street had been left open. This was his chance!

I'll just go for a quick sniff, thought Pierre.

He slipped through the crowd, out the door and followed his nose to the nearest park.

Pierre chased squirrels. He dug holes and rolled in anything he pleased. He even made friends! By the time he remembered Miss Murphy, it was dark.

Pierre rushed back to the big stone building with his new friends, Sparky and Lou. But the building was closed.

Where was Miss Murphy?

What should he do?

"Stay with us!" suggested Sparky and Lou. So Pierre followed them back to the park. That night his tummy rumbled, and he jumped at every sound.

"I want Miss Murphy," he whimpered.

The next day, Pierre dug into a buffet breakfast.

"Woo hooo!" he howled as he rooted through garbage with Sparky and Lou. Soon he was a glorious mess.

But Pierre had not forgotten Miss Murphy. After one last yummy morsel, he said good-bye to his friends. He could hardly wait to get home and see her.

Pierre sniffed here, he sniffed there. He looked down street after street. He circled around and doubled back only to end up where he started.

"I'm lost!" he cried.

Pierre scurried through the crowd on the sidewalk, hoping to find Miss Murphy.

But people shooed him away, even when he wagged his tail.

It was so cold Pierre wished he had his coat, hat and boots. When he thought about his cozy cushion, his full dish and Miss Murphy's warm lap, Pierre gave a long sad howl.

"I was the luckiest dog in the world!" he cried.

That evening, Pierre was scrounging in an alley for supper when he saw something pink flash by. He raced to the street and saw a familiar pom-pomed scarf disappear into a cab.

Miss Murphy?

Pierre ran and ran. Each time the cab slowed down, he caught up, until the car zoomed out of sight.

"Noooo!" cried Pierre. He couldn't lose Miss Murphy again! But then Pierre realized he'd smelled these streets before.

Pierre was off once more, and this time he followed his nose home. He slipped past the doorman, bounded up the stairs and skidded to a stop at Miss Murphy's door.

"ARRROOOOOOOOOOOO!" he howled.

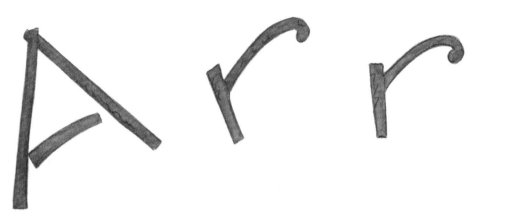

Arro

o

"What's that racket?" asked a neighbor.

"Some filthy mutt," said another. And they began to drag Pierre away.

Miss Murphy's door opened.

"Wait!" she cried. She pinched her nose and peered at Pierre. He was covered in garbage—chocolate syrup, chewing gum, fish guts and fries, bottle caps, bits of paper, spaghetti and cheese, sticks, twigs, grass and leaves. A piece of tissue hung from his tail like a flag.

"This couldn't be *your* dog," said the neighbor.
Pierre knew what to do.

With his scruffy tail high, Pierre walked perfectly, he stood perfectly and he held his head just the right way.

"Pierre!" cried Miss Murphy.

After hugs and licks and wiggles and wags, Miss Murphy gave Pierre his supper and a bath. Then she set his comfy cushion in the big bay window and snuggled in beside him.

Pierre nestled closer.

If he'd been a cat, he would have purred.

The next day, Pierre brought his coat and hat to Miss Murphy.
He held out a paw for each of his cozy boots.

"I was lost without you," said Miss Murphy. "I'm so happy
you're home."

Pierre gave her a great big lick.

He was happy too.

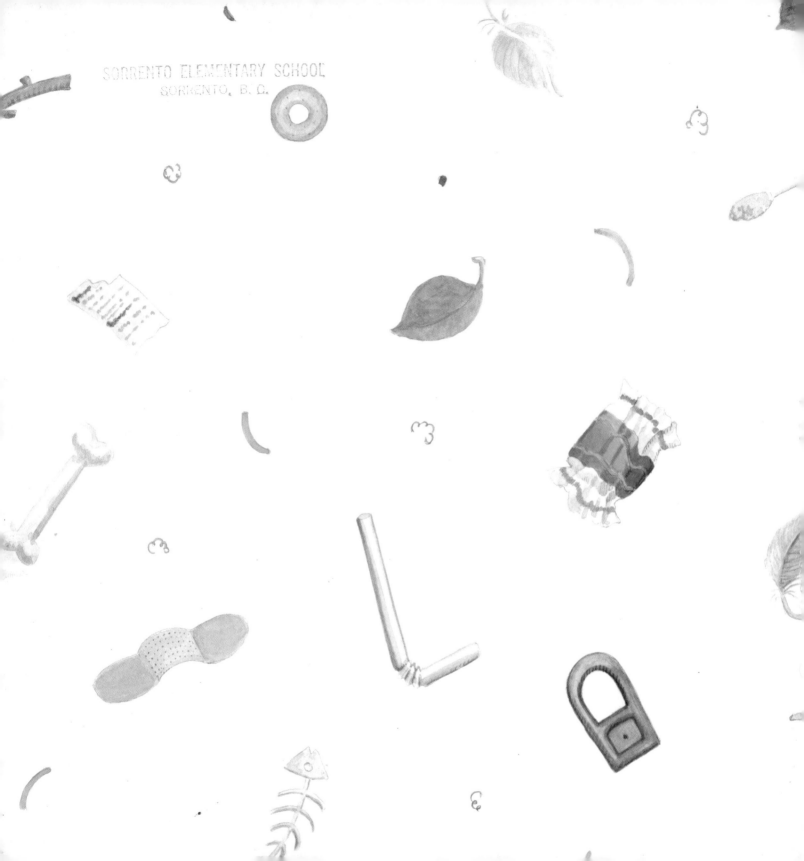